NASHVILLE NOIR

PARANORMAL MYSTERIES IN THE MUSIC CITY

A COLLECTION OF
SHORT STORIES
COMPILED BY
PARTHENON PRESS

Parthenon Press
Nashville, Tennessee USA
www.Parthenon-Press.com

To Nashville

CONTENTS

FOREWORD

Let me tell you a little of the background of how the work you have in your hands came about. If you call yourself a Nashvillian (by birth or transplant) and love to read, you should be proud to know that this city is full of wonderful writers just waiting to be discovered. Music City is home to the largest writers group on the Meetup.com network. To date, over 1100 writers are signed on to this assemblage. Not all of them will ever be published, but each of them loves the craft of writing and has a story to tell.

Last year, the leaders of this organization wanted to put together an anthology to showcase some of its best authors. What came about after months of hard work by many volunteers was 'Soundtrack Not Included' (published April 2012). Its blurb stated, *"This anthology represents a vision of what our group is becoming and will become. Short stories, poems and personal essays are presented within our first collection of member-written works."*

I believe it was a great start in that it showcased many undiscovered authors. And I'm not just saying this because an excerpt from my novel is the first work in the anthology. But, if you ever get a chance, please check it out. One hundred percent of its sales go to support this group.

It had only one real downfall, which was its size and scope. It was too large for one volume and there were too many genres between its covers.

Fast forward to this anthology. Inside the Nashville Writers Meetup Group, there are smaller gatherings that meet once a month. They range from fiction, sci/fi, memoirs, screenplay, etc. I myself attend three different ones and it has helped me tremendously to have a group of fellow writers review my ongoing projects.

Every year during the month of October, the leader of the fiction group at the time, Nikki Nelson-Hicks, would hold a contest to see who could write the best short story for Halloween with Nashville as the backdrop. Each year the subject of these works would change. One year it was vampires, another zombies. Once we even had to write in the style of H.P. Lovecraft. They all had to be under 2500 words with no names on them. It was a blind vote by the members and we were all on the honor system that you could not vote for your own story.

We always look forward to this competition because many of us were working on long works of fiction – *I was in the final edits of my first novel at the time* – and needed a break to prime the creative pump so to say.

The last year of this event the genre was Fiction Noir with a paranormal twist. We tried our best to mimic the styles of writers like Dashiell Hammett, Mickey Spillane, and Chester Himes. Being a horror/paranormal fantasy novelist, I decided to try something that I had never done – a comedy in the first person in the manner of Garrison Keillor's series of radio stories about a detective name 'Guy Noir'.

After the reading and voting that night, I thought the works were just too enjoyable to let them go unread. I wanted to share them and their authors with a larger audience. By that time I had started a small publishing venture, which I had developed to showcase my new series of vampire urban fantasies, The Holy Damned Saga. I had the ability to put together these short stories in a small anthology, so I collected them for publication.

What you have before you is the full compilation from that night, with very little editing on my part. I hope you enjoy them as much as we did.

A. Jay Lee
September 2012

P.S. The last story in this anthology was the winner of the contest. I have always heard 'you need to leave them laughing.'

Overnight Success and the High Price Thereof

By Luke Woodard

When my cellphone rings, I'm in the tub, soaking the bruises from a bar fight with a gang of vampire bikers.

"Malachi Swift, metaphysical speculation."

"Oh, Mal, I've really done it this time."

Madame Olga is Nashville's premiere psychic medium. Her real name's Peggy Guthrie. She's a total fake, but the best ones always are. Either way, I'd let her "read my palm" anytime.

I towel off while she fills me in. Someone came in for her super-deluxe package: *Sell Your Soul To Be A Star,* a theatrical séance where Peggy summons the gods of Country Music, who will bless you with success. All for $375 and your eternal soul.

"So this girl from Minnesota comes in with her parents. I do my whole spiel." She switches to her Bela Lugosi accent. *"No, you don't know what you ask. Don't gamble your soul for fame and fortune. Take your daughter back to St. Paul."*

I can just see her pushing the people toward the door, dramatic as a Mexican soap opera. She plays 'em until they're begging her to take their money.

"So I run their credit card and take them down to do the show. The next day, literally overnight, little Sherry Young is on the radio with a hit song."

I'd heard the song during my bath. WSIX played it, said it was a Youtube hit. I didn't hear what the big deal was. Over-produced track with an auto-tuned girl purring "I'm Not Too Young." Didn't do nothin' for me 'cept make me miss Loretta Lynn.

"Well, what's the problem, Peggy?" I say, pulling on my jeans. "You've got a bona fide success you can brag about."

Peggy huffs into the phone. "An hour ago, the parents call me all freaked out. They say there's something wrong with their kid."

She asks me to go check out the situation. They're staying at the Opryland Hotel under the name "Jones."

♪

"Who is it?" a voice says from the other side of the door.

"Malachi Swift. Peggy–I mean, Madame Olga sent me."

The door opens just enough for me to slip into the room.

"Thanks for coming, Mr. Swift." Jerry Young is pudgy and sweaty. His pudgy wife, Terri, is sitting on the edge of the bed. They're both jumpy, like they're waiting for the weasel to pop.

"Well, what seems to be the problem?" I say in my old cop voice. I look around the room, but don't see the girl.

"Our daughter, Sherry Young – you may have heard of her – she's not been herself since we left Madame Olga's. She's..." Jerry's mouth keeps moving but the words can't find any traction. I decide to try the wife.

She takes a deep breath and the words spurt out all at once. "There's something evil inside her. She's still my little girl, but she's...she's doing things."

The door to the room opens and the parents flinch like cats. Sherry glides into the room. She can't be more than thirteen but she's dressed like a college freshman majoring in sluttery. She's carrying something small between her hands.

"I found this downstairs by the boat ride." She spreads her hands and I can see the top of a bird's head bobbing.

"No, Sherry, please don't," her parents plead.

Without expression, Sherry crushes the bird. Her parents cover their mouths and look to me with wide eyes.

Sherry turns and moves past me with the dead bird.

"What are you going to do with that?" I ask.

"Put it with the others," she says as she pushes the bathroom door open with her hip. In glittery letters across her backside it says *Not Too Young*.

I follow her into the bathroom. The tub is lined with dead animals. A cat with a broken neck, a squirrel with a smashed skull. Two Pomeranians lay side by side, both with jaws broken, eyes gouged.

"Who's dogs were those?"

"Our dogs. Gary and Larry."

She slides the cat over and places the bird. There's no hesitation to touch dead things. Not a good sign.

I ease toward the door. It locks from the inside, so I'll need to improvise. Sherry snaps her head in my direction just as I slip out. I hold the knob as she strains against me on the other side.

We use a belt to keep the door pulled closed. I can hear a crowd gathering outside in the hall. Someone's spotted Sherry and word's spread, people wanting autographs and pictures.

"Why'd you let her go out?"

Jerry lifts his arm and shows me the bite marks.

"Oh," I say. "Well, for now keep her locked in the bathroom. I'll call you." They both nod and stare at the bathroom door. From the other side, Sherry starts singing her hit single.

I'm not too young, no, I'm not too young...

♫

Madame Olga operates out of a broad two-story on Music Row. She takes me down to the séance room where she performed the ceremony for the Young's. I see the problem immediately.

"When did you put this in?" I ask, pointing to the 10-foot laser pentagram on the floor.

"About a month ago. Replaced that neon piece of crap. We put the table and chairs right inside the symbol. Creeps people out – bright red star of Satan – they love it."

With an iPhone app, I calculate the angles. "This is a perfect pentagram." I'm careful not to step inside.

Peggy puts a hand on her hip. "It better be. The

guy charged me enough." Her face is done up for tonight's clients, but she's wearing hot-pink sweats under her long silk blouse.

When I explain my theory, Peggy rolls her eyes like a Southern Baptist in science class. But I'm sure about what's happened.

I call Jerry and break the news.

"So what do we do?"

"Bring her back her to Peggy's – I mean, Madame Olga's. I'll have everything set up when you get here."

♫

The parents arrive with Sherry wrapped up tight in a sheet. She's thrashing and foaming as they carry her into the room. Nashville's latest sensation is a full-on demon-possessed she-devil. (Probably not the first time that phrase has been used.)

"Mr. and Mrs. Young, I think I can persuade the demon to give up your daughter and go back to hell." They just stare at me while their daughter writhes on the floor at their feet. I should really ask for a check right now, while they're motivated.

I drag the girl into the center of the room and tell Peggy to fire up the lasers. The blood red pentagram blinks to life with little Sherry in the center. The parents take a step back.

"That symbol opens a door to hell?" Jerry asks, staring at the star on the floor.

"Like I said, because the measurements are perfect, it creates a spiritual 'soft spot' where the membrane to the next dimension is stretched thin. Thin enough for an entity from the neighboring realm to push a little magic through."

I slide the séance table into the pentagram right over the girl. Sherry arches and hisses. The demon sees the underside of the table where I glued about a hundred little silver crosses.

Next I move to a five-gallon bucket where I've soaked a sheet in holy water. In one motion, I pull the sheet from the bucket, flip it out and let it fall over the table. It hangs to the floor, hiding the girl from view.

The crosses and the holy water will trap the demon and hopefully make it so uncomfortable, it'll turn and run the only direction it can: back through the membrane. The more distress we can cause, the more it'll fight to return to the other dimension.

"Mommy!" the girl cries from under the table. Mrs. Young covers her mouth at the sound of her daughter's voice.

"This is a good sign," I tell them. They both look like they're on the verge of a stroke. "If she can cry out, that means the demon's pulling away."

But then the demon takes over. The harsh voice sounds like breaking glass. "We made a deal, Peggy!"

The great Madame Olga is pressed against the far wall, her mouth hanging open. She's still in the bright pink sweat pants with her enormous teased-out gypsy hairdo. I'd laugh if I wasn't busy ripping open an entrance to hell.

I grab the bucket and throw the rest of the holy water onto the table. The demon howls, then the girl's voice returns.

"Mommy! Daddy! I'm scared!"

"It's okay, Sherry," I say. "Just do what I say, alright?"

The demon wrestles back control. "I'm not going anywhere. I'm staying. You can't make me leave."

Mrs. Young buried her face in her husband's chest. He looks at me, terrified. I get Peggy's attention.

"Any ideas?" I shout. The demon's growls are shaking the walls.

Peggy looks at the table, then back at me with a shrug. I guess it's all up to me.

I scan the room for something, anything that might drive the demon back to the other side. Something so irritating, something so excruciating…

"Sherry!" I shout. "Sherry, can you hear me?"

Between demonic growls, her voice breaks

through. "Yes, I can hear you."

I roll the dice. "Sing!"

The parents look at me with a flash of fresh horror:

Dear God, our exorcist is on crack.

"Come on, Sherry," I yell. "Sing your song!"

The first trembling notes squeak out.

I may look like just a kid

"Louder, Sherry!"

But I'm a woman where it counts

"Keep going!" Her voice gains strength.

I will get all in your head

And turn you inside out

The demon tries to break in, but he can only gasp between the lyrics.

I'm not too young, no, I'm not too young

I'm not too young to rock your world

The floor begins to vibrate beneath our feet. The girl's singing voice is awful–just as I was hoping. She has all the musicality of a muskrat.

I'm not too young to be your gir-rl-rl-rl

The parents hit the floor and cover their heads as the room starts to quake. Peggy hunches down against the wall. The pentagram sprays a shower of sparks.

With a bellow that splits my skull, the demon roars in defeat. The pentagram blazes then fades, leaving the room dark and quiet. I can hear the parents whimpering. Peggy lights a candle and creeps my way.

"Mal? Is it over?"

I stand up and pull the sheet from the table. Sherry peeks out, shivering, soaked with sweat and holy water. I give her my hand and pull her to her feet.

The parents rush to their daughter, pulling her tight and kissing her soggy hair extensions.

Jerry sidles up to me, staring at the burnt-out pentagram. "So, her singing drove the demon out?"

I shrug and nod.

Jerry clears his throat. "Well, you know, this isn't a proper venue. No mic, no monitors. And nobody sings without auto-tune these days. That's just a fact."

♫

After the Young's leave, Peggy and me sit on the couch upstairs with a bottle of Jack.

"So you get $375 for pretending to contact to the spirit world, while I cast a demon back to another dimension and don't even get my expenses covered."

Peggy slips off the sweats from under her gypsy blouse and lays her long legs across my lap.

"And what did I tell you about conducting séances on the summer solstice? You're lucky your little laser show didn't let something even worse come through."

She bats her ridiculous fake eyelashes. "Sorry, Mal. Can I make it up to you?"

"Maybe I can get my palm read?" I hint.

She leans in. "What if it costs you your eternal soul?"

"It's all yours, Madame Olga."

Parthenon Press

Detour

by Nina Fortmeyer

The ancient captain puts me out at a riverfront dock.

The busy street leading away from the pier is unlike any I've ever seen. Enormous traffic lights hang over cars that look straight out of Captain Video films. Squarish buses are covered in pictures. How does anyone see out windows with pictures?

Yet it's oddly familiar. The buildings, that's what it is. If I ignore the strange lampposts and the crazy signs, it's Nashville. Broadway. The sign even says so, but it's a weird copy of the street where I pounded the pavement seven months ago, when I got here with a pocketful of LB's jack.

Except not here. Nashville.

I stand dripping, amazed to be alive. I thought I was a goner for sure, except Jinx didn't want me dead. He was just carrying out orders from LB, who was not amused that I made his moonshine drop and kept going west instead of coming home. He's never taken kindly to anyone who rips him off.

Maybe I died. Nobody could live through getting tied up and dumped off a boat into the Cumberland River. That's it, this is some kind of weird passage, a mix of this world and the next, except it's full of people who don't look dead. Just chubby and crazy, talking to themselves, holding up little boxes like the kind dames carry cigarettes in. Like they've lost their marbles.

At least I ditched Jinx and Fred. No sign of them anywhere.

I follow the sidewalk, pleased to find the path to the Pearly Gates lined with neon signs and bars. I can get a goodbye shot of Paul Jones, find a dry cigarette. I pat my damp pocket. No smokes, which wouldn't be good anyway. No money, which would be.

Nothing, not even the key to my flat.

I turn on 5th at a crazy round building, then see another weird building with a really big sign on the side.

Billy Lee, it says. Huge letters. And below it, a picture of me.

I pinch myself. It stings.

I stare, dazed, while a throng of people pour off a pink bus. I get swept into the Country Music Hall of Fame with them, across a really tall lobby to an elevator meant to look like a barn.

I want to wake up now. Please.

We get off the elevator and troop into an exhibit room. It's all about me.

Displays show the story of those late night sessions with Jock and Terry. People crowd around a glass case with my harmonicas inside. My guitars are there too, even the old crummy one Grandpa Lee gave me when I was eight, before my fingers were big enough to play the chords. A mother reads to her little girl about how I was born in 1927 and grew up in Robbinsville, NC, how I came to Nashville in 1945 fleeing a powerful moonshiner.

How *The Right Side of Love* was my first number one hit.

But it only just started getting airplay. If it went to number one, why don't I remember?

The last I recalled, I was at the Rainbow Room when a long legged dame sidled up to me sounding like home. Her sultry voice spilled like molasses onto the polished wood bar.

I tossed back the rest of my drink. "Another Paul Jones and one for the dame."

"Make mine a Rum Collins." The mountain lady edged closer. "Don't have nothing like this back in Robbins –" She stopped and turned away, facing the stage where Boots Randolph was tearing it up on the sax.

My heart sped up. "Where'd you say?"

"Robbins. Missouri. Come on, let's dance." Her red crystal bracelets caught the glimmer of the lights as she led me to the dance floor. I wasn't sure how I'd scored a babe like Lydia but I intended to enjoy it, especially when she asked me to walk her back to her hotel.

"I'm a little worn from traveling." She had a sweet titter of a laugh. "And cities scare me at night."

"Nothing to be afraid of." I loved her Smoky Mountain voice. Just like Robbinsville, where I couldn't go, not 'til I could pay LB back.

Music spilled out of the clubs into Printers Alley. She chattered and I drank it up. Her crystals caught the glow of the street lamps, disappearing when we stepped into a dark space between the lights.

"Hold me, Billy Lee." She clutched my hand and said my name kind of loud. My real name, not the one I'd been using.

Missouri, like hell. I dropped her hand and bolted.

WHAM.

Somebody cold cocked me from behind, then grabbed me. I staggered. A shadow shot out of the dark and snagged my other arm.

"Keep going and don't turn around." Two iron-firm grips forced me forward, the deep voice sounding for all the world like western NC. I hollered and locked my legs, making them drag me.

"Shut your yap, Billy." The thug on my left plowed his fist into my mouth with a flash of painful light. I knew that voice. Back home. Yeah. I'd been with Stella. Short, dark, not a looker like Lydia, but warm and easy. The dance after the Harvest festival when we snuck out and got interrupted in an uncompromising posture, this was her brother, oh crap. Jamey. No, Fred. Or Lonny. She had a million brothers.

I tasted blood.

Lydia opened the door of a Hudson parked on Church Street. Stella's brother shoved me into the back seat. I swung wildly, yelling, while he tried to squash me into staying still. No way was I letting him get hold of my other arm.

"Drive, Jinx," he said.

"Can't you shut him up?" Jinx's cackling laugh made me want to clock him, except there was a knee in my back, squashing my innards into places they weren't meant to go.

Stella's brother shifted his weight, forcing the wind out of me. "Come on, gimme your other paw." He pushed down harder. I tried to breathe but he was crushing my lungs.

"Just tie his ankles," Jinx said. I heard the car start.

"If I don't tie his hands too, he'll untie 'em."

Jinx wasn't the brightest bulb on the Christmas tree. A dumb, redheaded giant, he dropped out in sixth grade. We had been friends as kids, lost touch after he quit coming to school. Weird shit happened around him, creepy stuff. He made one of his cousins fade and come back. His whole family was freaky like that, all them redheads living back in Sully's Holler.

"Don't see why LB wants to bump Billy Lee anyway," Jinx said.

My heart leapt onto the floormat. There wasn't room for it in my chest anyway, with Stella's brother on my back. If this was LB's doing, I was toast. Mr. Big Money always got what he wanted. Rumors flew about the people who disappeared, but he never went to court.

"I'm gonna pay him back," I squeaked with the last of my breath, dizzy. White stars swam around the Hudson and the world went dark.

I came to with my wrists bound behind my back and my ankles tied. Jinx carried me out of the car onto an embankment.

"You about killed him," he said to Stella's brother. He set me down, then pulled a rowboat out of the brush at the edge of the Cumberland River.

"Ain't trying to. In fact, we got a change of plans, Jinx. We're gonna bring this boy home to his lady."

Who?

"Can't do that, Fred. No, we're gonna do exactly what Mr. LB said, then go home."

"I'm the brains here, Jinx. We're taking him back to Robbinsville."

Jinx raised his gun, a crazed look in his eyes. Truth be told, we stopped being friends because he scared me, making his cousin go invisible. I didn't care that he couldn't read or do math like everyone else did. It was the things he could do that drove me away.

"Don't ever call me dumb," he said, aiming at Fred's head. "We're doing exactly what Mr. LB said." He turned to me. "Don't you worry. Everything's gonna be okay."

Which is a weird thing to say while carrying somebody bound at the wrists and ankles into a rowboat in the dark. I wriggled, trying to knock Jinx

off balance. Fred shoved me down and smacked the back of my head.

"Do that again and you're dead meat," Jinx said, looking past me at Fred. "Me and Billy is friends." He began rowing rhythmically, the moon highlighting his huge shoulders, repeating "It's gonna be okay," with each pass like he was keeping time.

"You could let me go, Jinx. Stay with me in Nashville. It's a wild city." I was pretty sure Jinx didn't want to kill me, but he'd never move away from Robbinsville either. I was surprised he'd strayed this far.

"I'm taking this one back home, Jinx." Fred kicked me between the shoulder blades.

"Naw. It's gonna be okay," Jinx said, putting down the oars.

"For who," I whined.

"You'll be okay," Jinx repeated one last time and rolled me into the cold, dark river. I took a deep breath and kept it 'til my lungs were full of freezing fire, ready to burst. I held on as long as I could, then sucked in the cool river water. Blackness filled me and changed to light, really bright. I opened my eyes to a blue sky.

I was lying on something hard, moving. A boat, bigger than the one Jinx tossed me out of. An ancient redheaded man turned me on my side. I threw up water, coughed up water, took a deep breath and coughed some more.

Then I filled my lungs with blessed air.

The ropes Fred tied me with lay on the deck. I rubbed my chafed wrists.

"You're gonna be okay," the man said in an accent that made me think of the mountains. He led me inside the boat's small cabin, where he put a blanket around my shoulders. I wore it until he put me off at the dock.

♫

People smile for tiny cameras next to my guitars, my clothes and my harmonicas. Somebody raided my flat, whoever has my key. I'll have to get the landlady to let me in. If go to sleep, maybe the world will make sense when I wake up.

I can't place the song that's playing but it's me and Terry singing. The poster says it was our biggest hit, *Detour to the Future*, an oddball, funny song that propelled me to fame. I wrote it in 1947.

Only I walked out of a bar into Printers Alley in 1946 and got tossed into the Cumberland River.

The bio says my wife Stella and I had our first child that year, a boy. No wonder Fred was itchin' to take me back. And Jinx was our roadie? Too weird.

But if Billy Lee did all this, who am I? I look down. Sure enough, I'm wearing the same clothes I wore to the Rainbow Room, still damp from the unplanned swim. I'm trying to find a mirror when a lady in orange sabots stops me.

"Wow. You look exactly like him." She points to the life-sized cardboard cutout near the entrance.

"Distant relative, ma'am." I stand next to it, proud to pose for a fan even if it doesn't happen until I'm dead. I tip my hat, the same one as in the picture, then head to the other exhibits to find out which of my buddies made it big.

A firm grip on my arm stops me. I turn to see a red headed giant of a man holding the key to my flat.

"Not yet," Jinx says in a voice dripping Smoky Mountains. "Time to go back home."

THE UNANSWERED CALL

BY NIKKI NELSON-HICKS

I fell hard inside the phone booth, keeping my hand squeezed up against my guts. It was the only thing keeping them where they belonged.

"Operator. 5551879. Reverse the charges."

The ringing clanged inside my skull. I shook my head as my vision began to tunnel. The vertigo brought me back in time to hear the click of the connection.

"James?"

"Ricky!! Sweetie, where have you been?"

Doris. Just my rotten luck. "Doll, put James on."

She hummed along to some stupid song that was playing in the background. "I've missed you, sweetie."

Christ. "Get James. Do you hear me? Get him now!"

"He's not here, handsome. But I'm here, all alone."

I leaned against the phone. The cool metal kissed my swollen jaw. "Where is he?"

"I don't know and I don't much care!" She clicked her tongue. Jesus, what piece of work. It didn't take much for me to imagine her lower lip quiver as she pouted and stamped her size 5 champagne pink stilettos. My partner, James, was dizzy for the dame but, to me, she was dust. "James is such a grouch. He packed a bag and split right after you left." I heard her gasp. "Oh…God. Ricky, do you think he knows?"

Not this mess again. One sloppy New Year's romp and this bird pegged us for the next Bogie and Bacall. "Don't be loopy. There's nothing to know so stop bumping your gums about it."

"Don't be that way, Ricky. I'm lonely. I need you.."

"Not as much as I need James. Find him. Tell him I am at Percy's at 555-1478. Sing that back to me. Good."

"Rick-!"

I hung up before her voice drilled me another hole and sat down on the wooden seat. Warmth flooded over my hands. I closed the door with my foot. The winter damp was beginning to creep into my shoes. The Nashville Arcade was empty. Not a pigeon in sight. Beside the phone booth, Percy's Shoe Shine Shop was dark. It was strange seeing it so hollow. It looked lifeless without the hustle of suits waiting for their shines.

Outside the Arcade, Fifth Avenue was quiet. Maybe the goons hadn't followed me. Maybe they had given up. Or maybe they were just a block over in Printer's Alley waiting for me to surface like a rat from the gutter. Either way, no reason to get hinky with an ambulance siren. I'll just wait it out for James.

Where was he?

He had sent me on a box job. A simple can opener, nothing fancy. Crack the safe, get the goods and get out. A clean sneak. James owed an old friend a favor, he'd said. He passed it on to me because-

"You got the touch, Priest. The tumblers just fall underneath your fingers, don't they, pal?"

I never got to find out. I was copped before I laid finger one on the box. Palookas sapped me on the conk. I came to tied to a chair with two lugs using my mug for batting practice. A double breasted bull polished his badge while he asked me where I'd hidden the stash, who had hired me to steal it. Nobody wanted to hear my patsy sob song. The bull worked me over good and played my ribcage like a xylophone. I tasted copper long before he finished his first scale.

Lucky for me, his thugs weren't boy scouts. Their knots were weak. At the first sign of an intermission in their fist concerto, I made a break.

I didn't see the gun but I felt the bullets all the same. They drilled straight through my back and out my gut.

I ran through the streets until I made it to the Arcade, to the phone booth besides Percy's. James knows this place. We get our shoes shined for a nickel here. We act sweet to the girls down at the Peanut Shop and get free bags of hot nuts. He knows where to find me, knows where to call me. If only that dingbat can find him in time.

James, what the hell was in that safe?

So many questions. How did such a simple gig go south so fast? James said he cased the joint for a week. It was supposed to be empty. I barely got my nose in the door before they swooped down on me like so many crows.

'*The tumblers just fall underneath your fingers, don't they, pal?*'

I felt a cold stab in my kidneys. I coughed and spit up blood. The echoes of a deep, slow beat came towards me from a long tunnel. My head swimmed with the idea.

He packed a bag and split right after you left.

Dammit. My head is spinning.

God, I'd kill for a deck of Luckies. My lungs are aching for a drag. Then, I could think straight. Not be getting my guts wadded in my garters thinking up crazy Chinese angles like James hanging me out to dry. He'll call. The phone will ring, anytime now.

What if-

No...don't even start down that line. He doesn't know anything because there's nothing to know! Break it up...stop right there. We're like brothers, James and me. We drink from the same bottle. We're on the square. He'd never send me to get bumped off by a couple of Brunos. He'd never just lam off and leave me...

But-

Just ring, damn you! Ring!

James knows. Dammit, he knows.

I'll call Chesty. Sure. Chesty. He just lives over the bridge, owes me a fin from last week's card game. He'll come and we'll call it even steven. Everything will be golden.

But...I can't reach the phone. My arm, my legs. Feels like I'm coated in cold lead. My gut. There is more blood than shirt now. So cold...so cold. I can't move. Have I frozen stiff? Can that happen so fast? No, don't be a galook. No, it's not...not...that. Tired. I'm just tired. That's all. I can barely see. Are my eyes open? Make the call. I can't. Just...reach.

He knows. Sweet Jesus, James knows... oh god.........help me... Why won't the phone ring?.. Please... just... James... I'm... didn't... mean... I... am... so-

BRRRRRRNG! BRRRRRRNG!

"What the hell?!?" Terrance Donaldson looked down at the man shining his shoes. "What was that?"

Kel looked up at the young man sitting high in what his daddy used to call 'the Businessman's Throne. "What's that, sir?"

BRRRRRRNG! BRRRRRRNG!

"Didn't you hear that? It was like an old timey telephone ringing right next to my ear. I nearly spilled my latte!"

Kel rolled an eye over to Chester, a shoe shiner who had worked in Percy's since Noah set down his ark. "Did you hear anything, old man?"

Chester sat in an empty chair as he waited for another lunch hour middle management stooge to blow in from the Arcade. He kept his eyes on the television as he rolled an unlit cigar in his mouth and silently cursed the new no smoking laws. "It ain't nothing to worry about, mister." he said. "It's been doing that since Kel's daddy's time. Don't know where it comes from."

"That's just crazy. There has to be a reason."

Chester shrugged. "We mostly just ignore it."

STREET WINE
BY SUSAN BURDORF

It was fate that I found Robert Pascall first.

Hounded by police night and day, rousted from park benches or verdant grassy parks, we never got to rest undisturbed.

Robert deserved these few moments of respect from his friend before the indignities of removing evidence of his life took over and defined him.

So, when I found Robert's slightly ripe corpse lying in the dirt and grass next to his last bottle, I squatted near to him, but not *too* close, and lit a cigarette. I offered him one, but he silently declined. In his condition one more puff would not have killed him; but I respected his wishes and took a long drag in his memory.

It was a shame about the bottle though. I would have liked to have taken a drink in honor of his passing, but since drink is what got both of us into living on the streets of Nashville in the first place, I figured it was probably just as well that the bottle had shattered.

As I smoked and squatted I looked him over. I shivered as I felt a chill as if someone had walked through me. For a moment I imagined I saw Robert sitting with me, his familiar cocky grin disappearing into the air like that of the Cheshire Cat.

I shook my head to clear out the image and looked at his supine body with a critical eye. He deserved my best effort. But I couldn't shake the feeling that I was being watched and judged. Robert, in life, had been like that. He would fix you with a long stare until you revealed everything to him, then close it up inside an imaginary bottle and never mention it again. You could trust him with your secrets.

The first thing I noticed was that his hair was messed up; blood and gore from the brain matter had mixed with the maggots into a strange kind of living hair gel, turning him into an eerie Halloween-ish caricature. Quite in season, since it was late October. The rest of his clothes were dirty and torn in places, as if there had been a struggle. He had not looked like this the last time I had seen him. For a man who took care of himself and his appearance in life, he seemed to have let himself go in death.

I could also see that his skin was growing slack; rigor mortis was already gone so I knew he was at least twenty-four to thirty-six hours a corpse. In my former life, as a homicide detective in Des Moines, I had seen many a body like this, but none of them had I called friend.

A further look around the body and the area nearby revealed a rock, tossed into the grass, with a brownish stain, most likely the murder weapon. Its rough surface would hold a fingerprint so I left it alone. In the soft dirt around the body I saw the faint impressions of footprints pointed toward the city. Ridges of the treads were edged with Robert's dried blood.

I took another long drag from the cigarette and then stubbed it out on my boot, putting it in my pocket. No sense leaving evidence to direct the police's attention my way. It was then that I noticed Robert's sneakers were missing.

Shame, they were brand new, issued just last week from the Nashville Rescue Mission. I had not been able to get a pair myself, my boots still having usable life left in them. We both understood I would get them if anything should happen to him.

Guess this qualified.

A few minutes later the Cart Woman, Robert's lady friend, joined me in my vigil. If she had a real name I did not know it. On the streets we tried to keep some things to ourselves, a kind of protection, which we only revealed to those closest to us.

We did not speak, but continued to look at Robert as his skin slipped a little more from his bones.

More figuratively than literally, of course.

She pointed to his bottle and sighed.

I nodded in acknowledgement. Going to her cart she retrieved a bottle of discarded liquors she had collected and a couple of used paper cups, and we drank to his life.

No words passed between us.

Sometimes words just got in the way.

The alcohol was warm as it made a fiery path down to my empty stomach. I tasted a combination of scotch and gin mixed with some cheap wine, and smacked my lips in appreciation. "Street Wine" we called it. A blend of whatever was left over in discarded bottles that often littered the streets of Nashville.

She looked over his corpse and reached in to his pockets, careful not to disturb his clothing, and found there was nothing. I had already checked, but understood her need to be thorough.

"He was a good man," she said quietly, squatting next to me, the only evidence of deep emotion the cup she crushed in her hand. I was surprised to hear her voice, a raspy growl that was punctuated by a slight lisp caused by the space where her front teeth used to be. She did not speak much, and I was not sure I had ever heard her voice before.

She had come to the streets from a women's shelter after being used as a punching bag by a former boyfriend. Usually she avoided all conversation, using gestures and hand motions to communicate. I knew that she and Robert had been especially close, mostly in a non-sexual way. Both recognizing the brokenness in each other and the need to be with someone, but not have the responsibilities that a romance would bring.

Comfort on the streets was different for us than for other people. We did not need the physical release of a sexual coupling as much as we needed the security that a friend who watched your back could bring.

I had failed Robert in that regard, as evidenced by his rotting corpse. I hung my head in shame. I had been gone for several days on a personal journey that had kept me away as I had wrestled with my demons.

The Cart Woman, sensing my mood swing, had touched my arm. Her squeeze, while not an invitation, was welcome. I understood her needs as well as my own. I could tell that as we sat by our friend's corpse we were passing the torch, as it were. Taking from each other what we could, when we could, and accepting its limitations.

Robert was almost a visible presence with us. I turned quickly, thinking to catch sight of him just out of my view, certain he was there, not lying on the ground in front of me, but standing tall as always, but saw nothing. I felt a breeze brush my cheek and imagined it was Robert acknowledging my loss and comforting me. I reached up to touch my cheek, hoping to find it was his rough worn hand instead, but of course it wasn't.

I smiled ruefully; Robert would not appreciate my melancholy when there was a job to be done.

I stood up and brushed off my worn jeans. I held out my hand and lifted her up also. Chivalry was not dead on the streets. We both stood there a moment remembering our friend, each lost in our own silent eulogy, and then I started to walk away.

"I'm going to the Nashville Rescue Mission now. I'll call the police from there," I told her, "you might want to disappear. Robert will be okay, they'll take care of him."

She nodded and gathered her things to leave. "Talk to Johnnie Red," she whispered in her cigarette-burned husky voice. "Bobby told me to tell you that."

I looked at her in surprise. Did she feel him here too? I could see his smile again and cleared the fog in my brain that the rush of alcohol, even diluted as this swallow had been, always caused.

"When?" I asked confused, "when did he tell you this?"

"Before I came. He told me to come here and tell you this." She saw my consternation and smiled, her missing teeth making her smile childish and innocent of guile. "He said, 'tell Joe that Johnnie Red did it.' He told me to tell you my name; then he left." She looked away, lost in memory for a moment, her hand touching her cheek as I had mine just moments before.

Perhaps Robert had comforted us both as he passed by. I liked the thought of that.

"I'm Lizbeth," she continued, holding still for my reaction.

I nodded, accepting her offer.

Her trust.

Knowing that Robert would have wanted it that way made it easier to do.

"I believe you," I shared with her. She nodded, accepting my comments as if they were a contract. Both of us knowing that we were now on a different level, but that there were no expectations; just a promised connection.

When I got to the Rescue Mission I found Father Ryan and told him about Robert. I assured him I had not touched the body. There was no need to mention the searches in his pockets; we had not disturbed any evidence so why bring on trouble? It was bad enough I had found the body and been his friend; I didn't need to give the police any more reason to suspect me in his death.

While I waited I went outside to smoke a cigarette.

I joined a group already huddled together on the side of the front entrance. I acknowledged them with a nod and took a long pull on my cigarette, letting the smoke out slowly as I studied Johnnie Red.

Johnnie was tall and massive, a Viking-like man with his shaggy red hair and barrel-chested torso. He looked back at me with a sidelong-glance, confused by my scrutiny then looked away guiltily.

My eyes traveled from his rumpled jacket, to his thin flannel shirt unbuttoned to reveal a thick thatch of graying red hair, then down his patched and threadbare pants until my gaze rested on his white sneakers.

Robert's white sneakers. I recognized the small reddish-brown stains on the toes of the nearly new footwear and sighed.

It never failed.

Murderers, intent on their own agenda, almost always forgot the most basic tenet of the perfect crime, *clean up after yourself.*

It had been my experience that those who were caught were most often caught because they forgot a key piece of evidence, *themselves.* I had once solved a nearly flawless murder because the killer had forgotten to take off a watch when committing the crime. The blood spatters in the band had convicted him as clearly as if the corpse had stood up, pointed, and said, *"He did it."*

I tore my gaze from Johnnie and watched as the police cars pulled to the curb, lights flashing and sirens going. Father Ryan came out and stood with me. I put my cigarette out on the bottom of my boot, and stood tall.

Fate comes for us all at some point.

Johnnie, looking at me out of the corner of his eye, seemed to shrink as he realized, without a word passing between us, that I knew what he had done.

He shifted his feet and tried to slide by, but I put my arm around him and turned us both to the police officer as he approached. I pulled Johnnie forward,

and he hung his head, looking at his shoes with regret
as he accepted my embrace and his fate.

PHANTOM OF THE OPRY: A COUNTRY WESTERN NOIR

BY A. JAY LEE

It was 'All Hallows Eve' in the city that really needed its sleep and I was making time at one of the local watering holes when she walked in. She looked like she has stepped just out of the Roy Rogers and Dale Evans Show – which was not unusual here in the bright lights of downtown Nash Vegas. But it was *how* she was barely wearing it that would have gotten her thrown off that show by Dale herself. First, the rodeo shirt she was hardly donning looked two sizes too small for her curvy bust and if any of its buttons shot loose she could put an eye out in more ways than one. Second, her miniskirt that appeared to be no more than a leather belt with tassels was so tight that she must have jumped off a two story building just to get into it.

She spied me across the room and walked right up in her white cow kickin' boots and pink cattleman hat that had never seen an honest day's work in the field. All the virile eyes locked on her libidinous frame as she crossed over in my direction and many a brew was lost over her stride along with numerous chaps' self-respect.

"Mr. Renfro?" She asked with that voice that said you could sleep with me if you only knew the words to the song. Hell, I only knew the tune, but with enough time I could hum a few bars.

"Who's askin?" I returned.

"I'm Dixie Star. I was told by one of the doormen at the Ryman that I could find him here. I just had to look for the tall drink of water that was holding up the bar."

"You must have had some queer parents to create a work like you and saddle it with a name like that." I said.

"It's my stage name." She answered. "Now are you Levi Renfro, private dick, or do I have the wrong handsome stranger?"

"Well, you found me. What can I do for you?" I wanted to ask 'to you', but we weren't on a first name basis yet.

"Well, Mr. Renfro…"

"You call me Levi, Little Lady."

"Okay… Levi Little Lady?…"

"No… Just Levi." I said. It seemed that Ms. Star had drunk the water downstream from the herd one too many times.

"Just Levi, I'm supposed to perform at tonight's Opry, but when I got to my dressing room to change I found some of my personal items had gone missing."

"What kind of 'personal items'?" I asked.

She leaned over to whisper in my ear, brushing her grill across my front panel and I could tell her high beams were on. "My unmentionables." She murmured.

"If they are unmentionable, why worry about it?"

"No, Just Levi, I don't think you understand… my undies have disappeared." She backed away from me to look me in the eye with her baby blue peepers.

"You've run out… that means that you're…" She put her finger to my mouth so I wouldn't say it and with her other hand she pulled down on her skirt.

"Yes, Mister. I'm riding bareback." She removed her hand from my chops.

"Then let me give you some advice. When you sit down, cross your legs."

"I don't plan on takin' a chair, but I can't go on stage like this. The whole front row would think that they made the mistake of walking in on a show at the Rainbow Room on Printer Alley." She shot back.

"Why don't get some more underthings before your act?"

"Both the Woolworth and Caster-Knott downtown were closed by the time I had to get dressed. I can't believe I was brave enough to walk all the way down here to find you."

I wanted to ask why she going commando before she changed into her show attires or why she just didn't change back before she came and found me. But who am I to question the actions of a damsel in dis-dress. But again she was a few sandwiches short of a picnic but she could lay a spread and I could mind the ants. "Why don't you just cancel your act?"

"Well, this is my first time at the Opry and if I cancel it could be my last. Besides, there was a note." She put her hand to her neckline and worked down between her sizeable Bonnie and Clyde to pull out a folded scrap of paper. I knew this billet doux had seen Heaven and as I took it all I could wish was that I could have its experience in the future.

It read:

Dear Miss Star,

I have taken some items that I know are very personal to you. Even without these bits and pieces you are still to perform at tonight's Opry. If you do not I will end your career another way that is much more unpleasant and painful.

Love,
The Phantom

"This information would have been helpful earlier." I said pulling myself away from the bar. "Well, let's mosey and take a gander at your dressing room." I fought my way through the smoke and the beer that hung like a morning fog over the Tennessee River. Grabbing my leather duster off the hook by the door I thought for a second and looked down at the woman I had in tow. "It's a cool night little lady... I think you may need this more than me." I handed it to her.

She draped it around her shoulders, not even bothering to put her arms into the sleeves. "Thank ya much. It was a little drafty coming here tonight."

I took my Open Range Stetson from the hook and placed it on my head. I thought for years about changing my style the first time I saw LBJ wearing it. But Hell, he was our President now and the Texas Rangers were still wearing them. I liked to believe I was still one of them even though my star was taken away from me years ago.

We made our way down the windy streets to the back door of the Ryman. Found it odd that if this was a show night that the alley wasn't full of performers having a smoke or taking one last shot of courage before they hit the stage. Even listening to WSM, I could tell when one of the artists had a little too much of the liquid valor or were too heavy on the Mary Jane. "You sure there's a show tonight?" I asked as I grabbed the stage door.

"Yes, it's just early." She returned.

I guess I had lost track of time in the honkytonk or my good friend Jack Daniels was playing tricks on me. Nonetheless, I walked into a dark room that was the backstage. "Which way to your dressing room?"

"It's not really a dressing room per se. This place is so small we girls have to all share." She led me back to a small room just off the green room.

The space was empty but for a small dressing table a few chairs along the wall. "Where did you have your stuff?"

"There was a loose board behind the mirror of the dressing table. I felt for sure that it would be safe there." She pointed to the area like I didn't know what a mirror was. I pushed the mirror and table aside and found the loose board she was talking about.

Pulling the panel aside I looked into the small hole. There was only a small stack of papers. "Great, it looks like another note from our phantom." I said as I reached in to retrieve the stack. "Looks a little large to be a simple note again... May be a manifesto." As I pulled the papers out, I found them to be hand written sheet music. "What do you..." but as I turned to look at the vision of busting out beauty that was behind me, she was gone and only my duster sat in a fallen mess on the floor. I picked it up and threw it over my shoulder and went to look for the missing starlet.

I went out to the backstage and then stuck my head into the dark greenroom. "Dixie, where the hell are you?" I hollered out, "...this is no time for games." As I turned back around there was an old man standing there in overalls and a push broom in his hands.

"Can I help you son?"

"Yes, did you see a cute looking woman in hat and boots and not much more?" I asked.

"The Ryman is closed. I should be the only one here tonight... How did you get in?"

I took me a moment to get my head clear to what he was asking. "... Dixie and I came through the backdoor."

"Who… that backdoor is locked. I checked before I started cleaning. I don't want some crazy walking in on me." He looked right at me like I was the crazy he was talking about.

I walked past him to check the door we had just come in and he was right. It was shut tight as a fiddle. "That can't be. I just walked through there."

"I can assure I locked that hours ago." He was now holding the broom a little off the ground with both hands like he was going to fend me off if I decided to turn on him.

"Listen, I came in here with a girl. She hired me to find something for her."

"And what was that something?" he asked.

"Well… a gentleman would say in mixed company."

"Well, this 'gentleman' better say before I call the cops."

He had me dead to rights, "She hired me to find …. her underwear?"

"Now I know you're fuckin daft." He took a few steps to the phone on the wall. "Just give me a few minutes and the cops will be down here with some nice men in white jackets with a nice sweater for you." He pulled the phone off the hook and tried to keep one eye on me as he dialed. He looked like this was the first time he had seen a freak show and he wanted a refund on his two bits.

Then I remembered the sheet music in my hand, "Wait, I did find something." I held it out for him to reach for.

With the phone still in one hand he dropped the broom and took the pages from my hand. He took a long look at them. "Where'd you find this?" He didn't even look up as he dropped the phone to fall free, its cord made it slam against the wall.

"In a hole in the wall, behind the mirror in the dressing room." I paused for a moment, not knowing what his next move would be. Now that he no longer had the broom in his hand and had never gotten ahold of Nashville's Finest, I knew I could take him with little effort. But just before jumped him I saw a tear come to his eyes. That stopped me. It was one thing to make a man cry by beating the shit out of him, but it was another to see an old man let the dams loose over some notes on a page. "What is it?" I asked.

"Me and Dixie wrote this song together."

"Dixie Star?! She was the one who brought me here tonight."

He finally looked up at me, "Couldn't be son... She's been dead twenty years now."

I couldn't stop myself and the flat-foot inside me took over. "How did you know her?"

He looked back down at the words on the page, "I played steel guitar for her band, 'Rebel Brigade'."

"Dixie Star and the Rebel Brigade... Now that's original." I said under my breath.

"We were in love. One evening after a roll in the hay we sat up all night writing his song... Well we wrote it between 'sessions' if you catch my meaning." A twinkle came to his misty eyes and his mouth turned up into a small grin like a pole-cat that had just sprayed a nosey coonhound.

It was hard for me to think of this old man in front of me as a horn-dog and it made my stomach turn just thinking about it. "I think I just threw up a little... yes, I can taste it in the back of my mouth." So I changed the subject. "How did she die, if it won't make you start the waterworks again?"

He looked at me like I just killed his huntin' dog and ate it in front of him. "Well, her manager at the time was her wife beatin' husband and the night before we were to go on stage here, she fired him and told him that she wanted a d-i-v-o-r-c-e. Just like that new Tammy Wynette song. That night we played that song for the first and last time right here on the Opry Stage. That good-for-nothing S.O.B met her in the alley out back and killed her." He paused for a second to collect himself and I wasn't going to stop him; the story was just getting good. "He's doing life at Brushy Mountain. The band and I couldn't find this song. After a few months of trying to rewrite it, I gave up and took a job here to see if I could find it. By band mates always thought that her husband had taken this song and destroyed it, but I knew it had to be here. How did you say you found this?"

"Well a woman claiming to be Dixie found me at a bar and asked if I could help her find something that was taken from her."

He smiled again. "Her underwear? That makes sense now."

I wasn't getting the joke. "Why?"

"She always had the fear of going on stage bare back and one time I had gone so far as hiding them after one of our interludes."

"So, the woman who brought me here tonight was a ghost?"

"Not a ghost… an angel." He hugged the sheet music like it was a long lost love.

I unlocked the door and made a quick retreat so I wouldn't be a witness to what would happen next. Whether it was a ghost or an angel that brought me his case, I knew I wasn't going to collect any fee. So I chalked it up as another strange night for Levi Renfro, private eye for 'the city that really needed its sleep'.

WHAT HAPPENED TO THE GIRL?

BY ANGELA TRUMBO

An unlit cigarette dangles from the homicide detective's lips while his right hand rummages through the pocket of his gray trench coat. As he reaches the bridge railing, he pulls out a square metal lighter. With a flick of his wrist, the lighter flips open and he touches the end of the cigarette to the open flame. The lid closes with a quick snap and he drops the lighter back into his pocket. He draws deeply from the cigarette several times as he stares down at the river flowing beneath the bridge.

Several moments pass with the detective's focus only on the water below. When he does make a move, it's to fish out a brushed silver flask from somewhere inside his coat. He unscrews the cap and takes a long swallow. His attention shifts from the river to the flask, holds there for a few seconds before he replaces the cap and places the container back inside his coat.

Without a sideways glance, the detective says, "This is how it went down. After I tell you, I'm done with it. Understand? I won't be around for questions, so listen up and listen good." He doesn't wait for a response before he begins.

♫

It's around midevening when I'm here on this bridge and in about the same spot as we are now. I'm looking at the water and trying to figure out why in the hell some little sixteen year old girl wound up floating face down in the river. Dead bodies showing up in our part of the river isn't a normal occurrence in Nashville, mind you. The ones we do find usually involve some drunken homeless person getting too close to the edge and then, well, last bath they'll ever get.

Aren't any marks on the kid and no drugs in her system as far as the lab could find. The family is pretty tore up and what friends she had tells me she always seemed happy. Her death is a total shock to everyone. With no other leads to go on, I find myself back here on this bridge. I'm ponder on what evidence we have, what we might lack, and think I'm alone in the task when some female voice speaks low in my ear.

"She didn't jump."

I do a quick turn to the sound and Mother of God! My eyes behold one of the finest pieces of ass I have seen in a long time. Too long a time, but that's my own doings. Can't see women if you don't go where they are. Anyways, damn if it doesn't take me a minute to even remember who I am and then another minute to think on what she just said.

She stands there in a tailored business suit, the jacket fitted to accent her waist and the slim skirt stops below her knees. The deep purple color makes her short hair, cut to frame her face, appear jet black. Her lips are fire engine red and curves around a cigarette in a way that makes me wonder how they might look curved around, well, never mind.

I say to her, "Who?"

She removes the cigarette and blows the smoke out from the corner of her mouth before she says, "The girl found in the river last night."

Now mind you, word hasn't gone out yet about finding the girl. Nobody alerted the media and, even if the hounds found out, they would be under a gag order – you know how tight the Captain runs his business.

So, all cool like I ask, "How do you know about her?"

She takes another hit off the cigarette and says, "I was there." Her little bomb shell hits the mark and she walks away. I'm hot on her tail when I hear the Captain on the car radio. He wants to know my twenty. Takes me but a second or two to lean in the window of the car to grab the mike and the dame is gone.

I go back to the same spot two evenings in a row with no luck, dame never shows. With no other leads or suspects besides the nameless broad with the killer body, we're batting zero on this gig. Finally, on the third evening when I'm about to call it a day, she puts in an appearance.

"Been looking for you."

"I know," she says and pulls out a cigarette from one of those dainty little cases dames like her carry in those small clutches they use to store their lady junk.

She holds the cigarette between two fingers and waits. My mind is a bit slow to catch on she's waiting for me to light her. Quick as ever, I dig out my lighter and flip it open. She leans slightly forward, puts the cigarette in between her lips, and draws the flame onto the end. A seductive glint enters her eyes when she looks up at me while she sucks on the cigarette butt. She straightens, blows smoke from the corner of her mouth, and licks her lips in a way that suggests she had done something else.

Okay, I know what you're thinking. But damn it, I can tell when a dame is coming on to me. And I'll also have you know her actions don't make a difference. Or at least I don't want them to.

"She wasn't pushed, if that's your next question."

"Actually, my next question is to ask for your name." I drag out a pad and pen, time to do my damn job.

Her eyes shift to the water as she brings the cigarette back to her lips and takes several puffs. "Mary Grace."

"Mary Grace. Is there a last name? Or is Grace the last name?"

I swear to God at the moment her eyes are about as dead as any corpse I'd ever seen. A sudden desire to be anywhere other than here with this dame makes me want to take a step back. She is quite the looker but damn if I'm not grateful when she turns from me to face the water.

"If she didn't jump and she wasn't pushed, then how she'd end up face down in the river?" I ask.

"She fell."

"So you're saying it was an accident?"

She turns to me and this time her eyes are very much alive and gleam with an eerie light.

"On the contrary, Detective. It was her choice."

"Her choice."

She smiles and nods. "Yes."

"And you were standing right here and didn't try to stop her?"

The smile never leaves her face. "Now why would I have wanted to do that?"

"She's sixteen for God's sakes!"

"It was her rite of passage, Detective. Just like it could be for you, too."

With her little riddle left to hang in the air, she walks past me. Her heels click on the cement bridge until they fade into nothing.

I don't say anything to the Captain about her. At this point, I don't even know what to say. Place a few phone calls to track her name, but no one's ever heard of her, which doesn't surprise me much. What I do know is the broad both gives me the creeps and makes me horny as hell.

Next evening and I'm back on the bridge. Part of me hopes she doesn't show up and the other part wants to see her again. At this point, I'm pretty sure I'm blowing the investigation – not going by the book at all. The dame's got me so tied up inside wondering about her being on the bridge, watching a little girl end her life and not doing a damn thing to stop her. No matter how hard I try to keep it just business, I can't stop thinking about the dame in ways I'm fairly certain will only cause me trouble. Of course, that is all before she tells me...what she tells me.

She's waiting for me this time. What a picture she makes, leaning out against the railing with her eyes closed and such a sweetness of serenity on her face. I've a strong urge to touch her; an arm, back, shoulder, anywhere as long as I make physical contact. Before I get the chance, she turns to stare at me with the blackest eyes ever. All I can think is what the hell and has she always had black eyes?

"Still chasing the dead, Detective?"

"Still trying to find out what happened to a young girl who had her whole life ahead of her to look forward to, Miss Grace."

She's busy opening her delicate little cigarette case when she pauses, "Did she?"

"What? Was she sick or something? What are you not telling me?"

"She wasn't sick," the dame says and smiles. She withdraws a cigarette, gently closes the case and places it back in her clutch. "And as for what I am not telling you...maybe you aren't asking the right questions."

The cigarette is already lit and in her mouth before I can dig out my lighter. While I got it out, I go ahead and fire one up and take a few hits. She stares down at the water and blows the occasional smoke stream from the corner of her blood red lips. When she removes the cigarette from her mouth, I notice her long, pointed fingernails match her lips. The color makes her skin the shade of paper white except for the slight rogue on her cheeks.

"I'll bite. So what are the right questions?"

Her sigh is the sound of a whisper. Without taking her eyes off the water she says, "If you were given the chance to live a different life. One beyond your wildest dreams and with more than you could ever hope to obtain in a lifetime, would you take it?"

"Hell yes I would. Wouldn't anyone? Wait. What's the catch?"

She laughs. "Always the skeptic, Detective?"

"Nothing's free, honey."

She nods, "Yes, you do have to earn your right of passage."

"You said that before. Right of passage. Something the girl chose. What is that?"

She steps closer and when she touches my arm, I swear to God it felt like every hair on my arm stands straight up. Her eyes bore into me as she says, "Are you sure you want to know the answer?"

"Does it explain what happened to the girl?"

"Detective, I told you before, nothing happened to her. It was her…"

"Right to passage. I know. I know. But that doesn't explain why she's dead."

She pats my arm and steps back. "Dead to some, alive to others."

"Dead is dead, Lady. Once you're dead, you're dead to everybody."

"As I'm sure you've been told many times. But, tell me, Detective, do you always believe what you have been told?"

"Not likely. Just like I'm not buying this mumbo jumbo you're trying to sell."

"Are you happy with your current life?"

"What the hell does that have to do with anything? We're not here to talk about me. I'm here to find out why a sixteen year old girl-"

"I'm fully aware of why you are here, Detective. Even if you aren't." Before I could speak she lays a finger against my mouth and says, "At least not yet."

She turns back to stare out on the water. "If you really want to know about the girl," she holds up a hand right as I'm about to tell her to get on with it. "Then you will have to agree to accept my offer."

Those words are enough to get my back up and remind me to do my job.

"Look, Lady. I don't take bribes. You can tell me now or down at the station. Don't make much difference to me."

"It's not a bribe. It's an offer. And it's only valid here and lasts for twenty hours."

She turns to me, "I'll tell you all you seek to know, but, as you say, nothing is free."

Now, I don't make it a habit to cut deals with witnesses or potential suspects for which this dame is both, but I admit my curiosity got the better of me. I bargain for the information on the girl, accept the offer, and, well, now I'm giving you what I can.

♫

The detective flicks the smoldering cigarette butt out to drift quietly to the water below. He reaches into his coat pocket and drags out the flask.

"What the hell," he says and drains the contents in one long gulp. He hurls the empty container over the edge of the bridge and it disappears into the night.

"The girl didn't jump. She wasn't pushed. She just... fell," and with those words the detective climbs up on the railing, spreads his arms wide, and free-falls toward the river below.

Red Lily and
the Oriental Flower

By D. Alan Lewis

Darkness surrounds me but I feel as if the brightest flames of hell have wrapped around this tired and aching body. Even with the clock showing three a.m., sweat pours out of me and fills my sheets. Sleep will not come this August night. Outside of my apartment window, three leaf-covered sticks sway with the wind, smacking against the wall. Their noise always comes in the same distinct pattern.

Smack and then a pause followed by two quick smacks. It took one night in this new dump for me to catch on to what the noise brought to mind. Smack … Smack, Smack. It sounds like a heartbeat. I find it relaxing, like a baby hearing its mother's heart

69

beating for the first nine months. It's a constant and gentle reminder of a time when there are no cares or worries about the scum that I deal with every day as a man who solves other people's problems. Lying here, I'm drawn to the notion that the noise is the heartbeat of the building. It is my mother and this room is her womb.

Tonight, the noise bothers me for some unknown reason. I listen and feel an uneasiness growing within me. The wind makes the branches move faster and smack harder. I struggle to understand why their noise fills me with dread, but then it comes to me. The heartbeat grows faster. My mother is growing angry but the distant rolling thunder tells me it isn't anger. My mother is frightened.

On top of the stifling heat, the air has taken on a different sort of darkness. Storm clouds on the horizon glow in the moonlight and drift slowly this way. Bright flashes of lightning illuminate them with brilliant yet brief splotches of red and orange. From my bed, I watch them approach Nashville like a foam-covered wave moving in slow motion towards an unsuspecting beach.

I've not seen a brewing of clouds and darkness this evil since I came home from the war after the Japs surrendered, six years ago.

The phone rings and I leap from the damp sheets. The cool wooden floor feels wonderful beneath my feet as I stagger to the dresser and lift the receiver. My unshaved whiskers scrape across the hole-covered microphone and the noise briefly drowns out the sobs of a woman. I recognize her the moment she speaks. I've been expecting the call.

"Meester Dietrich, he gone again. He just left." The woman said in thick Japanese accent.

Hisae Newton was one of those rare and beautiful Oriental flowers that had been plucked from her homeland by an American sailor after the war. Her husband James had been one of those fortunate sons whose fathers made sure he got the plum assignments. While others like me burnt under the Pacific sun and endured the monsoons and mud, Newton sat in Hawaii soaking up the good life. After a couple of atomic blasts, he went to Japan as part of the occupation force. He fell in love and brought his flower home, much to the shock of his family and friends.

"You say you know where he go?"

My body is aching but not as much as her heart. "Yeah, I think I do. Sit tight. I'll bring him home."

I dress with speed but stop and gaze out the window when the thunder returns. The opening line to a bad pulp book I read as a kid comes to mind. *It was a dark and stormy night.* The story was bad and ended with a monster loose on the city streets. I've always hated foreshadowing.

As my Studebaker roars through town, I think about my client. Mrs. Newton paid me a visit a week ago. In a crying fit, she said her husband was leaving at night only to come home hours later, tired and dazed. This would happen about once a week. Another woman, she thought and plopped down enough cash to keep me on the case for a couple of weeks with a promise of more.

Tired and dazed she said. It sounds all too familiar, I think as my car rumbles through the twists and turns of Green Hills. I know exactly where to look for the fortunate son.

At three thirty in the morning, parking is easy to find downtown. Despite the heat, I slip on my trench coat and fedora. I drop my pistol into the right side pocket and my other weapon goes into the oversized pouch on the inside. The sweat on the back of my neck cools in the stiff breeze and brings some much needed relief to the sweltering summer heat. I lift my eyes skyward and see the full moon. Dark clouds move to surround the white orb in an attempt to extinguish its glow.

It's never good to be without the moonlight in this part of town.

Following the sounds of jazz, I cross Church Street and enter Printer's Alley. A few men and their questionable companions dance and stroll from one establishment to another. Their laughter and merriment is a far cry from my purpose.

The door of the VooDoo Lounge opens and cigarette smoke boils out into my face. If the owner could get the patrons to smoke hickory sticks, they would have the perfect place to cure Christmas hams. After a few steps inside, the bartender sees me. He rolls his eyes as if to say, *oh no, not again.* On the back wall hangs a bright red door flanked by a pair of men sitting on stools. I know one, a brute named Jimmy Boy but the other is new.

I ignore whatever band is attempting to entertain the drunken masses and walk a weaving path through the tables to the guarded door. Jimmy Boy stays on his stool, watching as I approached. When his friend gets up, Jimmy Boy holds out an arm to stop him. This new guy won't have any of it. My right hand drops into my pocket and caresses the barrel of the .38 while my left tugs at the top two buttons and pulls the cloth back. My shirt opens enough to ensure he sees the silver cross dangling around my neck. His dead eyes lock on to the cross and the corners of his thin-lipped mouth twitch upwards.

"Dat cross supposed to scare me?"

"No" I answer in a flat voice. "Distract you."

New guy doesn't see the pistol in my hand until its butt smashes into the left side of his jaw. The cracking noise echoes through the joint. All eyes turn to me for a moment before returning to the band, women or drinks. Considering how fast he hit the floor and the lack of movement afterwards, I don't expect him to see anything for a while.

Stepping over the new guy, I approach the door and tip my hat. "Jimmy Boy."

"Dietrich." He replies and opens the door. "Careful. She's got another new one in there."

The corridor is dimly lit but I know my way. The hallway goes back to the far corner of the VooDoo Lounge. The voices and moans of the pay-as-you-go lovers fill my ears as I pass the private rooms that line the hall. The place reeks of bad perfume and sin. At the final door, I ignore the hand-painted sign that reads, *Knock before entering.*

Her private room is larger than many homes. Rich woods and gold-colored walls give a false sense of wealth and taste. The furnishings are typical for 1951. She doesn't like being out of style, not even by a year. The woman stands at the far end of the room, kissing the man I came to return to his heartbroken wife. Sparks and flashes of light burst from the union of their lips. Newton's eyes are lifeless. His arms hang at his sides and his body jerks like a freshly caught fish dropped onto a sun-baked pier. She, however, works the unnatural kiss with an unbridled passion.

Off to the side, the other new guy watches her deviant embrace with lustful eyes. He hisses at my intrusion and springs up as if sitting on a catapult. With un-natural speed, he runs towards me. He looks like the first new guy. Maybe they are brothers or cousins.

Tall, skinny and stupid would describe 'em both. I think. With the pistol back in my pocket, I interrupt his charge by drawing my other weapon.

The vampire, to coin a phrase, stops dead in his tracks about an inch short of the razor sharp point of my wooden stake. His eyes are wide and his breath stinks. His lifeless eyes study the dark brown and black colors that stained the first eight inches of my maple rapier. It's been used before, many times.

"Boys, would yawl just settle yourselves down now." Her southern belle voice is sweet and playful. I hate how danger always comes in pretty packages. "Nick, hun … you just go outside and let me talk for a minute."

Nick snarls as he walks to the door. I turn with him to keep the creature away from my back. Once he is gone, I hear giggling and my gaze returns to her.

She's naked and takes great pleasure in the effect it has on the weak-minded men she lures into her domain.

Her name is Lily. To say that she is the typical southern belle would mean ignoring the long raven hair, the bright red skin, and the brown, leather-like wings folded on her back. She's a vampire priestess whose youth and innocence were corrupted years earlier. Draining a man of his blood is child's play for her. She consumes their souls.

Newton stands wide-eyed and lifeless as she playfully runs a finger over his pasty cheek. Lily taps his shoulders with a finger and he obediently drops to his knees. His breathing is shallow and he looks half dead which is about right.

"Let 'em go."

"My heavens, why should I?" she asks.

"Because he's the husband of a client." I stroll towards her keeping a tight grip on the wooden stake, knowing I won't need it.

"Now, our agreement is that I get three a month." Her words are almost sung to me.

"Yes, we agreed you'd take bums and out-of-towners." I tap her arm with the stake. She rolls her eyes and steps aside.

"You keep changing the rules. I'm willing to play your lil' game, hun, but I can change the rules too."

"Speaking of which, you have two new guys. Our agreement was you only get three boytoys." I haul Newton to his feet. He stares at her, drool leaking from the corner of his mouth. I slap the poor bastard once and then twice before he snaps out of it. He's groggy, unsteady, and vaguely aware of who or where he is.

"You went and staked Georgie for getting hungry. And then Leroy … My big Leroy … well I had to put him down myself. His appetites were just too much." Lust fills her eyes and she appears to slip away for a moment into a darkness that sickens me to think about. "All those yummy appetites."

My hands guide the drained man towards the door but she stops him with a look. I can see Lily isn't going to make this easy. Her smile brightens when she sees my head bow and I concede.

"Alright. You get two extra this month." She steps aside with a big grin. "Just make them country music singers. Can't stand the twangy bastards."

Her typical pouty face appears, "They all taste like chewing tobacco and possums."

As I push Newton out into the hallway, I pause as she speaks again but her southern charm is absent. "Dietrich, you're not going to be around forever. What happens to your city after old age nullifies our agreement?"

"I don't know, little sister." I shout over my shoulder as I push Newton away from her.

But I do know. Thirty years had passed since I killed off the vampire coven, but their master's final act of revenge cost me her soul. The wrinkles of time were mostly plastered on my face these days, but her sweet, mischievous mug would always be eighteen years old.

I'll die someday but she'll never outlive me.

I'll make sure of that, but this wasn't the night for it. Tonight, I had to get the fortunate son home to his Oriental flower.

THE CASE OF THE PINNED UP KNICKERS

BY KATHLEEN KITTY COSGROVE

I was sitting at my desk, cleaning the gum from my shoe and watching the 5:06 pull into Union Station right at 6:30 when the sound of footsteps on pavement told me I'd better grab the Colt 38 and check the barrel. Most of the time what's on the other side of that door is trouble, and I mean with a capitol T and that rhymes with P and that stands for trouble. I don't look for it, but it looks for me, and usually finds me too, here, at my desk, in my office.

You see, I'm a dick, a private investigator, a gumshoe, a flatfoot, a sherlock, a bizzy, a tracer, a snoop, a shamus. My name is Sam Heart, but the folks around here call me Sam. When I say around here I mean Nashville, the home of bright lights and shattered dreams, beautiful music and ugly…well, some ugly things too.

What I could see from the other side of the glass was definitely *not* ugly. She had a shape like a real shapely dame and it was clear from her tight dress that she wasn't packing. I put the Colt back in the drawer and called out, "Door's open sweetheart, come on in."

She was even more beautiful than her silhouette, full red lips, an hourglass figure and silky golden hair that looked like gold silk.

"What can I do for you Miz…?"

"You can get me one of whatever it is you're drinking," she pointed to the glass of gin in my hand. "And put some ice in it. I like my gin cold and my men hot, if you get my drift." She grinned like the cat that swallowed a little yellow bird. I was tempted to grab her and kiss her, but she looked like more trouble than a big sack of trouble.

"So doll, how'd you get that blood all over your dress, you shoot someone?"

"Say, what kind of detective are you anyway?" she asked. "I'm the one that got shot. See the hole in my chest where my inside stuff should be?"

"All you broads think you're so clever, but I've seen it all before; you shoot your lover, put a hole in yourself and call yourself the victim."

"But I *am* the victim," she said, starting to cry.

"Here," I handed her my handkerchief, "blow your nose and spill your guts."

"But I have no guts, can't you see? I'm dead, and when I say dead I mean not living, deceased, a corpse, a used-to-be-alive person. Didn't you notice I came *through* the door instead of opening it?"

The broad was making sense now, but I still didn't get her angle.

"What do you want from me? Looks like you need an undertaker, not a PI, a dick, a gumshoe, a…"

She broke in with more crying, "It's not me who needs the help, it's too late for me." She finished her drink and handed me the glass, "More please."

She downed the next one like a man…like a man that drinks gin, and then she walked slowly over to the window. "I used to love to ride the trains, they're so connected to each other."

She turned back to look at me, "It's Little Johnny Knickers. They're blaming it on him. The cops have got him locked up tighter than a guy in jail. He didn't do it, I know, I was there."

"Well, if he didn't kill you, then who did?"

"If I knew that, I wouldn't be here, asking you for help. You see," she stopped and looked at the cigarette in my hand, "you gonna keep those all to yourself?"

I lit one and gave it to her. She inhaled. I couldn't take my eyes off of her, watching that smoke pour out of her like smoke from a thing that's burning.

"Go ahead," I told her. "You were gonna tell me how you don't know who shot you."

"I don't know who shot me." She dragged hard on the Camel. "It was dark, and the shooter was wearing a hat and coat."

"This is 1943 doll; everyone wears a hat and coat, even in August."

"You see, Little Johnny and I were in the bushes and this... person in the coat walks up and just shoots me. Little Johnny's knickers were up in a tree where I threw them, just playful like. Anyway, there wasn't time for him to get them down before the cops got there. I was laying there, on the ground, watchin' him trying to shinny up there and get them. I was saying, *'Run Little Johnny, run, don't worry about your knickers now'*. But he just kept jumping and grabbing and saying, *'Shit, this is gonna be real bad for my career.'* But anyways, he couldn't get a good foot hold, you know how that is.

By the time the cops got there, I was too dead to say anything, so they put the cuffs on Little Johnny and took him off... without his knickers."

"Ok, so the two of you were havin' a roll in the hay when…"

"No, not hay. Bushes, or a hedge, or maybe even a flower bed, but not…"

"Never mind all that, tell me about the shooter. Could he have been the blackmailer?"

"Say...how did you know…?"

"Doll, there's always a blackmailer."

"Well, someone's been getting backstage at the Opry and pinning notes on his knickers," she said, making smoke rings from the hole in her chest.

Then she walked over and picked the 38 off of the desk and pointed it at me. "Is this a gun in my hand, or are you just happy to see me?"

"Put that down and come with me"

"Where are we going?"

"To the Opry, it's show time."

♫

The cabbie that brought her to my office was waiting for us at the curb.

"I hope you don't mind," she said, "the only cab I could get was this dead guy."

"Hey, how many times do I gotta tell you, I ain't dead?" he yelled out the window.

"Sure you are honey, don't you feel a breeze where the back of your head should be?"

She whispered to me, "Look at the size of that hole in his head, you could hang drapes in there."

"No problem doll face, half the people in this town drive without their brains."

♫

The Opry is a mixed bag of rhinestones and cheap whisky; of dames with soft voices and stiff hair; of men with cowboy hats and big city type things.

Little Johnny's dressing room was now being used by Mrs. Maybelle Carter and her three girls. They looked innocent enough, but I smelled a rat, or maybe it was Old Spice. I knocked on the open door.

"What can I do for you, P.I?"asked Maybelle. "Why don't you take off your beige trench coat and wide brimmed hat and have a seat?"

"Thanks," I said. "It sure looks like you made yourself real comfortable in Little Johnny's dressing room."

"Say, are you accusing me of blackmailing Little Johnny so there would be a red herring into the investigation of the murder of his girlfriend and then murdering his girlfriend and letting him take the blame for it just so that I could have this dressing room?"

"You're real sharp for a dame, a doll, a skirt…"

"But I love Little Johnny like a brother. He promised that one day I can even perform on stage 'stead of just playing my guitar back here, in the dressing room and sewing sequins on his under drawers."

"You seen anything suspicious since you been here, in Little Johnny's dressing room?" I asked.

"You don't believe anyone here at the Opry could be a murderer do you?" she asked. "Why, we're just plain folk who like to sing, play guitar, go to church, read our Bible, drink our own homemade whiskey, beat our wives, put things in our hair to make it look like something other than hair and cheat when there's a good song in it."

"That's right," said the oldest girl, little Junie, who was dressing her dolls all in black. "Everyone here is real nice to us, except for that lady who comes in here and puts notes on Little Johnny Knickers' knickers, she was rude."

I could see that I broke this kid good. She was ready to spill her guts and I was ready to catch 'em.

"Tell me everything you know, kid, and I promise the feds will go easy on you."

"The feds?" she started crying.

"Why, you don't suspect little Junie of doing anything wrong, do you?" asked her mother.

"In this town, every man with a guitar across his back and song lyrics on a matchbook is a suspect." I said. "Every woman with a tune on her lips and an agent in her bed is a suspect. Every..."

"Ok, I'll tell you," yelled out little Junie. "It was Miss Bitsy, the one who owns the bar back behind here. She gave me the notes and a nickel and told me to pin them on, but I didn't kill anyone, honest. Don't make me go to prison."

"You're not goin' to prison. Just keep your nose clean and steer clear of drunks." I handed her my handkerchief. "Here, clean your nose."

♫

Our cabbie took us around the corner to Bitsy's Fuschia Lounge. It was real crowded and some guy was on stage yodeling so I shot him in the foot. I needed to get everyone's attention and that guy was askin' for it.

"Someone go get me Miss Bitsy," I said.

"I'm standin' right here in front of you P.I."

I had to look down to see her. She was three feet if you didn't count the hair, four if you did.

My ghost dame was standin' at the bar, hustling cocktails from a guy with a stab wound. The place was crawling with dead drunks. "Hey," I shouted to her. "This dame look like the shooter?"

"Who the hell are you talkin' to?" Bitsy asked, "Are you off your nut or somethin'?"

"Oh, didn't I tell you?" my client asked, "No one else can see me, just you and other dead people. Can we stay a while? I think the drowned guy over there is giving me the look over."

I looked back down at Bitsy, "Don't try to change the subject. I know it was you that was blackmailing Little Johnny. The kid you paid to do your dirty work sang like a canary that tells on people."

"Are you saying Little Johnny and me were lovers?" asked Bitsy. "That we used to roll around in the costume trunk and play *"hide the choo- choo in the tunnel*? That I found out that he was two-timing me with that floozy of a tramp of a floozy and ratted her out to her husband? That I'd been planning it all along and that's why I let the kid pin the notes on the knickers, so a P.I. would come along and think Johnny was being blackmailed?"

She pulled a gun from her brassiere, we struggled, the gun fired.

♫

I was sitting at my desk, scraping gum from my shoe when I heard footsteps on the stairs.

These two looked like trouble. She had a head of fiery red hair and he was packing. They began to argue and I could tell it was gonna be one of *those* kinds of cases.

"You can forget it," she told him without even lookin' my way, "It gives me the willies."

"It's not like he got killed here. He bought the farm down at Bitsy's. Beside's that why we're getting it for cheap. Now, sit down and type somethin'."

These two ain't got a clue what bein' a P.I., a sherlock, a bizzy, a snoop, a shamus, a flatfoot's all about. Looks like I'm gonna be busier dead than I was when I wasn't dead.

ABOUT THE AUTHORS

LUKE WOODARD (Overnight Success) writes music for a living and fiction for fun. His stories range from supernatural techno-thriller to subtle satire about religion. Born in Gary, Indiana but raised in Detroit, Michigan, he resided in the mountains of Virginia and the suburbs of Chicago before landing in Nashville. He is a fan of smart sci-fi, medium-rare steaks and four-part harmony. His son Logan recently surpassed him in height, but there's no need for you to point out this fact.

NINA FORTMEYER (Detour) is a fiction writer, enamelist and pastry chef. Her published works up to now have all been artwork and recipes. She is a member of Quill and Dagger writers group and Nashville Writers meetup, and volunteers with the mystery writers' conference Killer Nashville. She lives in the hills north of Nashville with her husband, four happy chickens and a peculiar dog.

Her sporadic blog appears at

http://cookingback2reality.blogspot.com/

NIKKI NELSON-HICKS (What was Done was Done) has been described by a fellow author as the "unholy lovechild of Flannery O'Connor and H.P. Lovecraft" and is burdened with the reputation as a damn good shag. She can be stalked on Twitter as **Nikcubed** or you can get more insights into her ever unfolding neurosis on her horribly neglected blog, **www.nikcubed.blogspot.com**. Inquiries as to her genetic origins or references as to her shag qualifications can be granted upon a request to **nikkinelsonhicks@gmail.com**

SUSAN BURDORF (Street wine) Susan Burdorf has been a member of the Nashville Writer's Meetup for the last several years. In that time she has been published in numerous anthologies and indie magazines for both poetry and fiction. A member of the Society of Children's Book Writers and Illustrators she recently was honored with an Honorable Mention in the Middle Grade manuscript category for a steampunk adventure novel that she is hoping to publish soon. You can reach Susan at susan.burdorf@comcast.net.

A. JAY LEE (Phantom of the Opry) was born in Cookeville, but within a few months of birth his family moved to Nashville. And except for a short exile to Memphis for a year and a half when he was too young to understand and the years he spent at the University of Tennessee, he has lived in Nashville all his life where he resides with his wife and three children.

A. Jay's debut novel, *Grace Through Blood,* is the foundation of a series of five books based on Jamie Grace and the Holy Damned, an order of quasi-Christian vampires that rule the nights in Charleston, South Carolina. To learn more about *The Holy Damned Saga,* please follow A. Jay at **www.Facebook.com/holydamned.**

ANGELA TRUMBO (What Happened to the Girl) is a fiction author who enjoys writing paranormal/scifi/thriller. Information about and links to her work can be found on her website **angelatrumbo.com**.

D. ALAN LEWIS (Red Lily and the Oriental Flower) is a native of Chattanooga, Tennessee who now resides in Nashville with his children. He has been writing and illustrating technical guides and manuals for various employers for over twenty years but only in recent years has branched out in to writing fiction. In 2006, Alan took the reins of a Novelists Group where he has been working to teach and aid aspiring writers.

Alan's debut novel, *The Blood in Snowflake Garden*

was a finalist for the 2010 Claymore Dagger Award presented to the best unpublished murder mystery manuscript. He has a second novel, *The Lightning Bolts of Zeus* being released in 2013.

KATHLEEN KITTY COSGROVE (The Case of the Pinned up Knickers) is a writer living in both Nashville, Tennessee and Naples, Florida. She has just completed the novel, *Engulfed* and is currently working on the follow-up to it, *Entangled*. Her short story, "Nku" appears in "*Soundtrack Not Included*" published 2012.

Photo taken October 2011. The night all these short stories were read for the first time.

Starting from top left corner moving clockwise around the table: Rick Jackson, **Nikki Nelson-Hicks**, Erin FitzPatrick, **Susan Burdorf**, **Nina Fortmeyer**, **A. Jay Lee**, **D. Alan Lewis**, **Luke Woodard**, Mandi Lynch, and **Angela Trumbo.**

Kathleen Kitty Cosgrove was taking the photo.

(Sorry, Kathleen. But you did win best story.)

38050975R00067

Made in the USA
Lexington, KY
21 December 2014